Ghosts

of

The

Illinois
River

For Janet —
It was such a pleasure to
meet you! Enjoy the stories, and
thanks for reading!! :)

Sylvia Shults
3/20/10

© Sylvia Schults 2010

"from ghoulies and ghosties, and long-leggedy beasties, and things that go bump in the night, the Good Lord deliver us." There are all kinds of bumps in the night to be found along the Illinois River. The river has seen centuries of history come and go, and has witnessed its share of mystery and dark deeds. Sylvia Shults is your guide on a trip down the longest river in Illinois. Come and meet the *Ghosts of the Illinois river.*

The reader should understand that we were able to obtain some of these stories only if we promised to obscure the actual identity of persons and/or property. This required us to occasionally use fictitious names. In such cases, the names of the people and/or the places are not to be confused with actual places or actual persons living or dead.

Dedication

This book, as with everything, is dedicated to my one, my only, my Rob. Thank you so much for your patience, and for understanding that sometimes, dishes just don't get done and supper can be very very late. This book was finished just before our tenth anniversary. Here's to ten times ten more wonderful years together!

Table of Contents

Ghosts of the Illinois River

Illinois is a very long state – tall, as states
go. From Chicago in the north, where I grew up, to
Golconda at the south end of the state on the Ohio
River, where my in-laws live, is halfway to the Gulf
of Mexico. And the longest river within this long
state is the Illinois.

If you kneel where the Kankakee and Des
Plaines rivers meet, about forty-five miles
southwest of Chicago, and push a toy boat out onto
the river, it will bob and float, beginning a journey
of 273 miles through the fields of Illinois. It will
float due west for a while, the light of the setting
sun glowing on its plastic sides. It will pass Ottawa,
the site of the first of the Lincoln-Douglas debates
in 1858. At Spring Valley it will turn and head
south, meandering a little more west as it goes. The
tiny toy boat will bob along, floating through Peoria
Lake, which is really a wide spot in the river, where
in 1892 the *Frankie Folsom* sank in a storm. Most
of the passengers survived the sinking of the
excursion steamer, but nine people from Pekin died.

Your little boat will float further downstream, passing the Meyers Mound site near East Peoria, where in 2005 a family digging out the basement for their new house found an Indian burial mound. It will pass the small town of Creve Coeur, named for Fort Crevecoeur, built in January and February of 1680 by Robert Cavelier, Sieur de la Salle, about a mile and a half downstream from a village of Peoria Indians. Fort Crevecoeur was the first structure built by Europeans in the territory. Because it is so light, the tiny boat will just bounce off of any branches it hits – unlike the steamer *Columbia*, which sank in 1918 in the worst disaster the Illinois River has ever seen. Eighty-seven people died when the *Columbia* went down.

The little boat will continue on its journey downstream, passing towns and drifting through counties as it goes. Your toy boat might get a curious stare from a fat, furry beaver as she goes about her business in the early dawn light. It might get a friendly bump from underneath from a playful fish. But it will keep on going, following the course of the swiftly flowing river. The Illinois is a highway for barge traffic, which has carved out a deep channel in the middle of the riverbed. A system of five locks regulates the height of the river and lets barges pass freely. The Illinois River is the most important water route in the state.

But the little boat is just taking a one-way trip, unlike the barges that travel the river. You'll be there to meet it when it arrives at the wide, flat beaches near Grafton, where the Illinois flows into the wide, placid Mississippi. You'll wade out into the wet, sucking sand and pick up the small boat, shaking the muddy water off of it. Your toy boat has finished its journey, but ours is just beginning. Come back up north with me, and we'll follow the river, picking up stories along the way.

Are you ready to meet the ghosts of the Illinois River?

Up In Flames

Let's start our journey down the Illinois River with a truly strange tale. There are no ghosts in this story, but there are two mysterious deaths, which remain unexplained to this day.

It was Christmas Eve, 1885. Patrick Rooney and his wife were celebrating the good cheer of the season.

"Another glass, m'dear?" Rooney hooked his finger through the handle of the brown half-gallon jug on the table, lifted the jug, and shook it playfully at his wife. She grinned across the table at him.

"Don' mind if I do," she said with ponderous dignity. "Go 'head and fill 'er up." She held out her glass, and Rooney tipped the jug.

Smooth amber liquid burbled out into her glass. She sipped it, and smiled again in appreciation.

The door flew open, and John Larson, the Rooney's hired man, came blustering into the kitchen, stamping his feet and blowing on his cold fingers. "Chores 'r done," he muttered. "Whoo, it's cold out!"

"Care for a tot of whiskey, John?" Patrick Rooney reached for another glass and poured a couple of fingers into the bottom of the tumbler. He handed the glass to Larson, who took it with a grateful nod.

"Get that down your gullet, it'll warm you right up. Cheers!" Rooney raised his glass.

Mrs. Rooney raised hers too, and clinked it against Larson's drink. "Cheers, an' Merry Christmas!"

"Merry Christmas," Larson agreed, and threw back half the whiskey in one quick swallow. He stayed up drinking with the Rooneys for a while longer, talking and laughing and sipping the strong, smooth whiskey. After two drinks, Larson stood.

"Well, Christmas Day or no, I've got chores to do in the morning. I'm off to bed."

Mrs. Rooney raised her glass once more as Larson headed up to his bedroom. "Merry Christmas, John!" he heard as he climbed the stairs.

Larson woke up in the middle of the night, coughing and sneezing. He found it hard to breathe, and in the dark of the night, he thought miserably that he might be coming down with a cold. He sniffed and hacked a few more times, then managed to drift back off to sleep.

He didn't feel much better when he woke up early the next morning, Christmas Day. His throat was still scratchy, and it hurt to swallow. He rubbed at his eyes, which were dry and itchy. He got dressed in the darkness of the bedroom. Maybe a glass of cool water and a breath of fresh air would set him to rights.

Larson made his way through the dark house to the kitchen. The bright yellow glow of the kerosene lamp would bring cheer to the gloom of early morning. He fumbled in a drawer for the box of matches, and tried to strike a match on the stove to light the lamp. But instead of catching with a satisfying skritch and flare, the matchhead just skidded smoothly across the cast-iron surface of the stove.

Puzzled, Larson ran a finger over the cold stove, then rubbed his fingertip against his thumb. The stove, and everything else in the kitchen, was covered in a greasy, sooty grime.

This is just plain strange, Larson thought. *I'd best wake the Rooneys.* He knocked on his employers' bedroom door. When no answer came from within, Larson bit his lip gently, then pushed the door open.

There lay Patrick Rooney, sprawled dead on the floor.

John Larson gasped, then shouted for Mrs. Rooney. But there was no answer. The house was still and silent in the early morning light.

Larson stumbled out of the house. He went to the barn, saddled one of the horses, and rode to the neighboring farm, where Patrick Rooney's son lived. He told the son of his father's untimely death, and together, they rode back to investigate further. By the time they arrived back at the Rooneys' farm, it was fully light out. And in the light of day, the two men made a horrifying discovery.

In the kitchen, every surface was covered in greasy black soot. Beside the table, there was a three foot by four foot hole in the floor. Underneath that, lying on the cold floor of the cellar, one floor below, was what was left of Mrs. Rooney.

She had weighed 200 pounds in life. But now, all that remained was a skull, a chunk of vertebra, part of a foot, and a scattering of ashes.

Even stranger, except for the greasy soot, there was no sign of the fire that consumed Mrs. Rooney and burnt a huge hole in the floor. One corner of the tablecloth was slightly scorched, but that was all.

The cause of Patrick Rooney's death was obvious. He had died of smoke inhalation. If John Larson hadn't closed his bedroom door before going to sleep, he might have died too. But the cause of Mrs. Rooney's death was not so easily explained. The coroner said that only a fire burning at over 2500 degrees Fahrenheit for several minutes could have consumed the heavy woman's body so completely. But no one, not the coroner, nor any other investigator, could explain why there was no other damage to the kitchen.

To this day, Mrs. Rooney's death remains a mystery. In modern times, cases like this one are explained by using the term spontaneous human combustion, a phenomenon described as "the high-speed consumption of a human body by intense heat, with no apparent outside cause".

Victims of spontaneous human combustion do seem to have a few things in common. They are often female, and they are often overweight. In many cases, the victims are found to have been drinking alcohol before their demise. The combustion, though mysterious, is usually rapid and complete, incinerating most of the body, and leaving only scattered body parts behind. Stranger still, nearby items are left untouched by the searing heat, even flammable materials like cloth. One more intriguing coincidence? Nearly all cases of spontaneous human combustion have occurred during the winter months in the northern hemisphere.

Scientists and paranormal investigators have tried and failed to explain spontaneous human combustion. It remains a mystery even today.

A Dog Named Tige

Mose Jenkins hugged himself as he walked, wishing that his threadbare coat had more of a liner, or fewer holes, or something. Illinois was cold! It didn't ever get this cold in Virginia, where he'd lived all his life.

But he wouldn't have stayed in Ol' Virginny, no sirree, not even if someone had paid him. He snorted, even though it warn't nothing to laugh about. Slaves didn't *get* paid.

Mose straightened his shoulders. He'd been a slave, but not no more. He was a man grown, sho 'nuff, and he'd decided to run North. Be free or die trying, he'd finally made his own choice, like a man.

He blew on his freezing fingers, and scanned the riverbank as he walked. Somewhere around here, if the directions he'd been given were right, there was a cave, a small natural shelter. He'd heard about it from a free black who'd taken him in for a few hours last night. Directions and a hot meal, and he'd been on his way. Mose didn't want to endanger his host any further than that.

"They's a cave, right down to the river," the man had said as Mose had shoveled down cooked kale greens and cornbread soaked in gravy. According to local information, Putnam County Cave was the exit point of an escape tunnel, one that started in the Putnam County Courthouse. Mose wasn't interested in finding himself in no courthouse, but he wouldn't mind catching forty winks, especially if it was somewhere out of the cold and wet.

There it was – a darker shape among the shadows on the riverbank. Mose stepped over some stones to the mouth of the cave, and pushed a bare branch out of the way. "This'll do," he muttered. He made his way into the cave, treading carefully, mindful of twisting his ankle on a stone in the pitch blackness. He felt around with cold hands until he found a mostly flat spot on the cave floor. Then he eased himself down, curled up, and tried to sleep.

A sound woke him up, a strange snuffling sound. He had been dozing, but now he was wide awake, bathed in hot sweat even in the freezing cold. Mose sat up and turned his head towards the mouth of the cave, just visible in the dim moonlight.

The snuffling sound came again, and now Mose could see a dark shape at the cave's entrance. It was a dog. He froze. He knew from stories and from bitter experience how dangerous dogs could be to fugitives.

The dog came sniffing closer, and Mose held as still as he could. There was nowhere for him to go. He couldn't flee further into the cave, because he had no light, and the dog was blocking the exit. Mose shut his eyes and prayed.

A cold nose shoved underneath his hand, and a warm wet tongue licked his palm, begging for attention. Mose laughed softly through his fright.

"You aren't gonna bark after all, are you? Maybe you's a runaway jes' like me."

Mose heard panting, and a wagging tail brushed the cave floor in front of him. In the dim moonlight, Mose could see the dark furry shape of the dog. It was a mutt, with a wide head and a dark brown ruff at its thick neck. It looked a lot like the dog that had hung around the slave quarters when Mose was growing up, the dog he had secretly named Tige…the dog he had thought of as his own.

Mose reached out and ran his hands along the dog's fur. He pulled the dog close, because it was warm and friendly and because it smelled so good. He buried his cold fingers in the animal warmth of the dog's rough-soft fur. A few tears leaked out from his closed eyes.

He started to lay back down. He patted the dog's side, hoping it would lay down with him to keep him company. The dog's body heat sure would be welcome, too. But Tige – Mose had already started to think of him as another Tige – nudged his nose into Mose's palm and whined.

"No, it's time to rest, boy." Mose leaned back and closed his eyes. "I been walking all day, I'm tired."

Mose felt a gentle tugging on the corner of his worn coat, and looked down. The dog had taken some of the threadbare material in its teeth and was pulling on it, the way the old Tige used to do with an old knotted hunk of cloth, growling and worrying at it while a young Mose play-fought him at the other end.

"Come on, I ain't playin' right now." Mose pushed the dog away, but it came back and grabbed another mouthful of homespun. It didn't growl playfully, but yanked with silent, dogged insistence, its back paws scrabbling on the cave floor.

"No, Tige, I can't, I *gots* to rest here," Mose whimpered. The dog growled softly and jerked its head. Mose heard a few soft pops as old threads gave way.

"Fine, darn you. Guess we'll find somewhere else to sleep," Mose grumbled. He got up and stumbled out of the cave. Cold wet raindrops stung his face. Before he could wrap his coat closer to ward off the cold, the dog grabbed his sleeve in its teeth and tugged again. The dog led him away from the cave mouth and into the shelter of some nearby trees.

Mose heard rough voices coming from the mouth of the cave, and saw the yellow light of a lantern bouncing off of the wet rocks. He ducked behind a tree and knelt down, pulling the dog to him to keep it quiet. His fingers sank into the dog's ruff as he bit his lip. He didn't dare run, not right now, they'd catch him for sure. All he could do was hold still, hold real still...

"I don't see no runaway slave," came a hard voice. "That tunnel's so narrow, there's no way anyone coulda got past us. There jus' ain't nobody here."

"Guess you're right. Whoo, look at that rain come down! It'll turn to snow within the hour. Let's just go back through the tunnel to the courthouse. Least we'll be dry that way."

A murmur of agreement, then the yellow lantern light faded. Mose let out a breath, which turned to mist as he breathed. "Slave catchers," he whispered. He hugged the dog tightly and buried his face in its warm, fragrant ruff.

The dog stood still for a few moments, then pulled away and woofed quietly. Mose got to his feet, and when the dog started walking, he followed it. As they walked through the woods, Mose noticed white flakes drifting down, spiraling to land silently on the forest floor. *Least they won't be able to track me through the trees,* he thought.

They walked for half the night, it seemed. Mose was dead on his feet, just stumbling along, when he realized they'd come out of the woods. Instead of trees, a forest of stone rose around them. Here, a row of granite headstones was lined up at neat attention. Over there, the falling snow piled up on the head and praying hands of a young angel. Her stone wings were already covered with caps of white.

"Aw, Tige, where'd you bring me?" Mose spoke in a voice that was half-whisper, half-moan. "I don' wanna walk through no graveyard." But the dog kept walking steadily. Mose had no choice but to follow. He stumbled through the deepening snow, cursing as the cold seeped wetly through the cracks in his brogans.

Then he stopped, his cold feet forgotten. There was a tall, dark figure blocking the path in front of him. An eerie yellow glow filtered through the phantasm's dark outline.

Mose's heart fluttered wildly, and the blood froze in his veins. He knew it had been a mistake to cut through the graveyard. Here he was, disturbing the dead on a cold snowy night, and now one of the spirits had risen to seek its revenge. The spirit lifted its arm, seeming to reach out for him –

-- and warm yellow light spilled from the lantern that had been hidden under the figure's greatcoat. The lantern lit the snow with a welcoming glow, and illuminated the figure's friendly face, creased in a gentle smile. The dog yipped and bounded over to greet the man.

"Are you in need of help?" The man was old and gaunt, but he was definitely human, and his voice was kind. "Don't be afraid. I'm a friend of a Friend."

The air went out of Mose's lungs in a sob of relief. It was the sign he'd been waiting for all these weeks of running. Conductors on the Underground Railroad were often Quakers, or knew of the Quakers – who were also called Friends. And they were friends to the running, frightened slaves who were trying to escape to freedom.

Mose nodded, the gesture made violent by the cold that still ate through to his bones. "Yes –

yes, I need help. I thought – thought – thought you was a haint," he said through chattering teeth.

"Oh no," the man chuckled. "No, I'm just the caretaker for the cemetery. I haven't yet joined my neighbors under the ground. Come on, let's get you in out of the weather and get some hot food into you." He turned to lead Mose to warmth and safety.

"Wait!" Mose cried, and the man turned back to him with a questioning look. "Sorry, suh, but can my dog come inside with me?" He owed the dog at least a hot meal and a warm place to sleep for the night. The dog had saved him from the slave catchers and led him to safety. And he did look *so* much like Tige.

The caretaker frowned. "I didn't know you had a dog."

"Yes suh, he right there beside you. He won't be no trouble, he's a *good* dog." The dog looked up at the caretaker, grinned, and thumped his tail in agreement.

"Let's get you inside," the caretaker said again, gently this time. "If we hurry, the snow will cover your tracks."

Mose looked behind him. In the yellow light of the lantern, he could see footprints in the snow, weaving between the gravestones in a stumbling path, leading off into the darkness. But there was only one set of tracks – the wide prints left by his own brogans.

The dog padded over to him. It licked his hand once with a warm wet swipe of its tongue. Then it loped off and disappeared into the snowy, trackless night.

Cemeteries and Other Spooky Places

Cemeteries. Graveyards. They are the resting places of the dead. But sometimes, the dead don't rest easily. And many burial grounds along the Illinois River have their own chilling legends.

Lacon is home to Old Salem Cemetery. One of the graves there holds the earthly remains of a young girl who died in a fire. To this day, it's said, it's impossible to light a match if you are standing anywhere near her grave.

The asylum at Bartonville had its own cemetery on the grounds. We'll pass over that graveyard for now, but we'll return to it soon enough, later on in this book.

Across the river and half an hour down the road from Bartonville is the tiny town of Tremont.

Mount Hope Cemetery can be found easily enough here. It's right in the middle of town, and as a matter of fact, the two paths leading into the cemetery look for all the world like someone's driveway, if you're not paying attention. Mount Hope is a large cemetery and many of Tremont's citizens through the years have found their final resting places here – but not all of them. Local legend tells of a family that lived outside of town a mile or so. The entire family was stricken with cholera, and the people of Tremont, fearing the spread of the disease, forbade them to come into town. Their gravestones can still be seen on a farm outside of town, several white stones forming a huddle against the green grass that covers their graves.

Returning into town, several of the graves at Mount Hope Cemetery have a unique feature. In addition to the headstone, quite a few graves are covered with polished slabs of solid stone, marking the outline of the grave. One of these large stone-covered graves is that of an organist for one of the local churches. The legend holds that if you kneel and put your ear against the stone, you can hear strains of ghostly organ music, as the long-gone musician still plays to her congregation.

Just outside Forest City is Zion Cemetery. This graveyard is quite small, nestled into a clearing in a wooded area. Zion Church once stood next to the cemetery, but it burned down in the mid-1950s. There are several whispered stories about this graveyard. It's said that when you first enter, you'll instantly feel a cold breeze. The cemetery is said to be haunted by the spirits of those unfortunate souls who perished in the church fire. (Although, truth be told, there are no records of any fatalities from the fire.) If you visit the cemetery after dark, you may hear the muted giggles of little girls at play in the woods surrounding the cemetery's iron gates.

But the most chilling of the stories about Zion Cemetery is this: at the back of the burying ground is a gravestone that sits next to a large, spooky tree. A former preacher of the Zion Church is buried there. If you knock three times on the trunk of the tree, the noise will reverberate down through the roots into his casket. And from his resting place, the preacher will let out an ear-piercing shriek at having his eternal rest disturbed.

Farther south and west is the dark, mysterious stretch of wilderness known as Effland Woods. This area, near Vermont, Illinois, was named after the family that once owned and farmed the land. The farmhouse where the Effland family once lived was up the road from the woods, although it's long gone now.

This little pocket of wilderness reminds us that Illinois was once all untamed frontier land, and that even the native Americans who lived here before us couldn't know all the dips and hollows and secret places of the forest. A small dirt road once led through these spooky woods, but as the years passed, the road was swallowed by the verdant growth, and it is no longer passable. Unexplained balls of light hover and skim through the trees.

A while ago, a young man went out into Effland Woods to hunt raccoon. As he left the house, his mom wished him good luck with his hunting. The boy came back about an hour later, very shaken and quiet. His mom, not realizing at first that anything was wrong, asked him why he was back so early. When he didn't reply, she noticed that he looked like he was in a state of shock.

The young man wouldn't tell his mother what had happened. In fact, he refused to talk about it at all, to anyone. The only thing he ever said was that he would never, ever go hunting in those woods again.

It was a hot day in July when I went to see Zion Cemetery for myself. The directions I had were a bit dodgy – one of the right turns was missing, and there wasn't a sign where there should have been – but after a bit of casting around and backtracking, I did find it.

I left the motorcycle parked close to the road and walked up the hill to the cemetery. Looking down as I walked, I could see a stampede of small critter tracks in the loose soil, which around here is more sand than good black Illinois dirt. The dirt was so loose and powdery, I couldn't tell if the tracks belonged to a dog or a deer, but there were lots of them. I could just imagine how hard it would be to dig a straight-sided grave in this yielding soil.

The white iron gates of the cemetery swung open with absolutely no sound at all. The only sounds I heard were the singing of birds in the woods all around the graveyard, and the crunch of my boots on the dry gorse underfoot. I had unzipped my motorcycle jacket before my trudge up the hill. As I stepped through the gates, I did feel a cool breeze, but I expect that was due to the wind at the top of the hill reaching fingers inside my open jacket to chill me. It felt good, actually. The thermometer that day was somewhere north of eighty degrees, and I don't care if you're wearing a mesh jacket on a motorcycle, in that kind of weather you're going to be hot, and you're going to sweat.

I picked up an empty Camel cigarette packet lying on the ground, intending to dispose of it later. I have a thing about litter, especially in a cemetery.

But as I looked around, I realized with a sense of cautious hope that that was the only bit of garbage lying around. I walked further in, and in the middle of the cemetery was a wire mesh garbage can nearly full of beer bottles and soda cans. I could tell two things right away: first, people weren't shy about coming to this cemetery to hang out. Second, they were respectful enough to clean up after themselves. I dropped the cigarette packet in the garbage can with a satisfied grin.

I wandered around the graveyard for a while, watching and listening. I didn't see anything out of the ordinary. The place just had the quiet, slightly melancholy vibe I usually associate with graveyards that aren't in actual use anymore. Many of the names, and even inscriptions, were German. I found several gravestones near big trees, but none of them seemed to belong to a man of the cloth. I suppose I could have knocked on the trees one by one and listened for the screams, but I didn't feel like being that disrespectful in search of a restless ghost.

A Chill In Chillicothe

"Your books are due on the 30th – that's in three weeks," Dominica said with a smile as she pushed the stack of books across the desk. She watched as the patron scooped up the pile of books and headed out the door of the library.

As the heavy glass door closed, Dominica reached under the desk and felt for the romance paperback she'd stashed under there earlier. She was so glad her library job gave her the freedom to read during the slow times. That was one of the reasons she didn't mind working by herself. The library in Chillicothe was small, so it really only took one person to keep an eye on things in the evenings. She settled back into her chair and opened the book with a happy little sigh.

The sound of a closing door, and footsteps, got her attention. She looked up with a smile for the approaching patron – then her smile faded. There was no patron in sight, no one browsing the stacks, no one coming up to the counter. Dominica shrugged and went back to her reading.

A soft thump carried over the quiet hush of the library. It had come from one of the fiction stacks. It sounded like a careless patron had dropped a book. Dominica sighed, put her book down, and went to investigate.

There was no one in the fiction aisle, but there were a couple of books on the floor. Maybe someone had shoved them through from the other side when they'd put a book back on the shelf in the next aisle over. It happened all the time. Dominica bent over to retrieve the books, and put them back on the shelf.

She headed back to the desk, but before she could get back to her reading, the quiet thump came again. She blew her bangs off her forehead in frustration, and went back to the stacks.

The same books had fallen off the shelf. Dominica could see the empty spaces on the shelf where she had put them just moments before. She picked the books up off of the floor for the second time, turning them to read the spine labels.

"Hmm. DER, DEM...Okay, I get it," she muttered. She ran her fingers lightly along the shelf. The books had been in the wrong place, that was all. She made a mental note to remind the page, who worked in the mornings, that Mrs. Armitage just hated it when books were misshelved. Dominica put the books back, making sure this time that DeMille came before Denniston. Then she went back to the desk, shaking her head.

Mrs. Armitage was kind of bossy for someone who had died in the 1980s.

"She actually hit me with a book once," Dominica told me. "I was shelving books in the Children's Room. There was some big book, like an oversized picture book – anyways, it was something you have to put all the way onto the shelf to get it to stay, you can't just shelve it carelessly. Well, I wasn't paying attention, and I put it in the wrong place. It just flew right off the shelf and smacked me low in the back, right above my tailbone. Mrs. Armitage just really doesn't like it when books are in the wrong place."

You could always tell when Mrs. Armitage was around by the smell of her perfume. Dominica told me that it wasn't obnoxiously heavy, just an old-lady kind of floral scent. But, she says, it wasn't something you wanted to smell without prior warning.

And oddly enough, she has another connection to the fussy phantom. When Dominica was a little girl, it was Mrs. Armitage who gave Dominica her first library card, starting her off on a lifetime of reading.

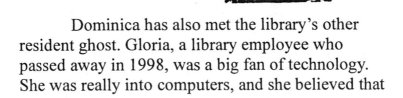

Dominica has also met the library's other resident ghost. Gloria, a library employee who passed away in 1998, was a big fan of technology. She was really into computers, and she believed that new technology was vitally important to libraries' growth.

When Dominica came back from college to work at the library in 1999, she was again working alone when she heard keys clicking at a nearby keyboard. She was far enough away that she couldn't see the keyboard from where she was sitting, so she got up to investigate. The noise immediately stopped. She sat back down, and the noise started again – the keys merrily clicking away, as if invisible fingers were typing on the keyboard.

"I don't think that was Mrs. Armitage playing with the keyboard, since she died in the eighties, before the library had a lot of computers. I really do think it was Gloria. It makes sense, because she was so into technology."

Chillicothe has since built a new library. The old building, where Dominica used to work, is now a used bookstore. The building has good bones, though. The floor plan is the same, and the store owner even kept some of the library shelving units to display his stock. Do Mrs. Armitage and Gloria still haunt the building?

Well, if you visit the bookstore and catch an unexplainable whiff of some floral perfume, or hear the phantom clicking of a keyboard being tapped by unseen fingers, you might decide that the answer – is yes.

The Curse of Old Lady Gray

The main branch of the Peoria Public Library stands at the corner of Main and Monroe streets. It's a chunky, modern building, a solid landmark amid the bustle of passing traffic. There is nothing there to suggest that this land is the focus of a curse that was uttered more than 150 years ago.

The land on which the library stands was owned by Mrs. Andrew Gray in the nineteenth century. Mrs. Gray was a crusty old woman who had worked hard to make a home for herself and her family in Peoria. But bad luck seemed to have it in for Mrs. Gray. Her garden failed year after year. The bitter Illinois winters were rough on her aging joints. And her nephew, who lived with her, was a lazy good-for-nothing layabout who was constantly in trouble with the law. The final straw for Mrs. Gray came when the nephew's lawyer, a young up-and-comer named David Davis, foreclosed on the Grays' property to settle the nephew's mounting legal debts.

On the day the old couple was to move out of their home, Mrs. Gray hobbled outside to the back yard. Raising her clenched hands to the heavens, she spat out her bitterness in a heartfelt curse. "May this land turn into thorns and thistles, and bring bad luck, sickness and death to its every owner!" Then she left Peoria forever, leaving the curse to fester.

David Davis soon moved to Bloomington and built a fine home there. He never lived in the property formerly owned by Mrs. Gray, and so he escaped the curse. But the other owners of the property were not so lucky. The curse would blight the lives of those who lived there, and later, worked there, for the next 77 years.

From 1847 to 1894, the property passed through five owners. The first family to live in the house after the Grays was the family of ex-governor Thomas Ford. In 1865, both of his sons were murdered. Soon after that, both Mr. and Mrs. Ford died – some say of grief for their boys.

The house stood empty for a while after that. One winter, in the middle of a blizzard, the house mysteriously caught fire and burned to the ground. People claimed that night to see the figure of an old woman dancing and capering in the flames.

Shortly after the Civil War, a freedman named Tom Lindsey moved a shack onto the foundation of the ruined house. A few months later, the shack was hit by lightning, and it too burned, a total loss. Lindsey rebuilt his tiny home, this time protecting it with a lucky rabbit's foot and a whole pile of horseshoes. He lived there for another 25 years.

After Lindsey's death, the property was bought by a banker. He built a grand house for himself, then married and brought his young wife to the home. She bore him a child, and they lived happily on the property – but within just a few months, the curse struck yet again. The banker's wife and child both died. A year later, the banker remarried, and soon afterwards, his new wife was pregnant. But this happiness was not to last either. The baby died soon after birth, and the mother had to be hospitalized in her distress.

The banker, broken, moved out, and the grand home was turned into a boarding house. Here, too, the curse continued. The woman who ran the boarding house lost two children – her son died in an accidental fall, and her daughter drowned in nearby Lake Peoria.

The Peoria Public Library bought the land in 1894, and began construction on its new building in 1895. The curse focused then on the directors of the library. The first director, Erasmus S. Willcox, was hit by a streetcar and killed in 1915. His successor, S. Patterson Prowse, was felled by a heart attack in 1921 during a heated board meeting. The next director, Dr. Edwin Wiley, lasted only three years at the job. In 1924, he poisoned himself with arsenic. Later, it was discovered that he had tried to kill himself at least twice before, and had at one time been committed to an asylum.

Mrs. Gray's killing curse seems to have lost some of its fury after that. But there is some evidence that the library is still home to several eerie presences. Mrs. Gray hasn't killed anyone in almost a century, but something still lingers in the building.

Linda Aylward was my guide one afternoon at the library, and she did her best, as a historian, to separate fact from fantastic fiction. Andrew and Mary Stevenson Gray did live in a house at 105 NE Monroe, where the library now stands. They were Irish immigrants who came to Peoria in 1833. Mary Gray was far from the stooped old crone of legend. She was a highly respected woman in the town, and she actually took in former governor Thomas Ford and his wife when they fell on hard times. Mrs. Gray lived comfortably in the house on Monroe Street for many more years than the stories say.

There was no "curse". But strangeness still surrounds the building.

There were several deaths connected with the library in the early years. The first director, a Mr. Solden, actually died before the property at Monroe Street was acquired. He was an avid bicyclist, and he rode from Washington to Peoria, a distance of about fifteen miles. He caught a cold from the ride, and died of pneumonia at the age of 39.

Mr. Willcox was the librarian who was responsible for purchasing the property and directing the building project in 1895. Linda showed me the picture of Mr. Willcox that hangs in the historical room. The portrait shows a distinguished-looking man with a full white beard and piercingly intelligent eyes that stare out of the picture. In 1915, he was well into his eighties, and mostly deaf. He wasn't looking where he was going when he stepped off of the sidewalk into the street. A trolley hit him and fractured his skull. And it is true that Prowse and Wiley followed Willcox into prematurely early graves.

Linda told me that there have been strange occurrences on every one of the library's five levels. The ghostly events usually happen to maintenance people or support staff who are working in the library very early or very late, when the building is closed to the public.

The basement of the library is a creepy, unsettling place of nebulous shadows and cold spots. One room is an orderly progression of row upon row of bookshelves that hold many old or historical materials. The face of an old, bearded man has been seen peering out of the window to this room. Is Mr. Willcox still watching over his books?

A librarian was working alone in this room – which has just the one door – when she heard her name being called from the darkness at the back of the room. Thinking that someone had come in and slipped past her without her noticing, she turned the lights on to illuminate the back of the room, then went into the stacks.

The lights went out, leaving her in the darkness between the looming bookshelves. She scooted back to the lighted area in which she'd been working, and huffed, "If someone's there, you'd better turn the lights back on!"

The lights did come back on at her irritated, frightened request. But the librarian was standing next to the bank of light switches at the time. It was an unseen hand that flipped the switches to illuminate the room.

Another time, an architect with the Philip Schweger firm was in a different workroom in the basement, working on archiving and filing architectural drawings. As he bent over the drawings, it seemed to him that he could see the apparition of a lady in a long black dress, hovering just at the edges of his peripheral vision, peering over his shoulder as he worked.

The administrative offices are up on the third floor. The staff break room is up there too, and one day, while several staff members were eating dinner, a foggy, cloudy, shadowy shape floated out through a closet door and across the break room. The diners were startled, but not surprised – apparently such goings-on aren't unusual. People regularly report hearing the sounds of doors opening and closing, when they are in fact securely locked. And it's not only strange noises, either. Linda told me the story of a security guard who was making his rounds one evening. When he came to the administrative office hallway, some of the doors to the offices were open, even though the staff had left for the day. The guard closed and locked the doors and continued on his rounds. When he got to the end of the hallway, he heard a series of clicks behind his back. He turned to look back down the hall –

--and every door to every office was standing wide open.

Some of the most spectacular ghostly activity at the library was witnessed by a staff member named Richard Partee. He was a janitor at the library for many years, and one night he and a few other workers were shampooing the carpet on the main floor of the library after hours. At about 2:30 in the morning, as they worked near the nonfiction stacks, three rows of books just came off of the bookshelves. "They came off one by one by one, just like some invisible hand was pulling them off the shelf and dropping them on the floor," Richard says.

Richard doesn't take any guff from the spirits, though. Once when he was in the boiler room, several rolls of paper towels floated out of a box one by one. Richard yelled, "Knock it off!" The towels fell to the floor, and he says he didn't see or hear any activity for six months or so afterwards.

But activity still continues. Curse or not, the Peoria Library is a haunted place. I spoke with a young security guard, Carl Dodd, who told me that one morning, very early, he was making his rounds and had gone to the basement to make sure that everything was secure. He unlocked the basement door, opened it, and was met with a rush of icy cold air and "a moaning sound that would not stop". He shoved the door closed and tried to lock it, but it wouldn't lock.

Carl still works at the library after that terrifying incident, but he said it best when he told me, "They're very angry ghosts...they're *mad.*"

Ghosts Are People Too

"Good afternoon, Peoria Players Theater."

"Hi there! I'm a local author working on a book of ghost stories, and I understand you guys have a ghost."

And that's how it started – my most personal and enjoyable ghost experience ever. I was about to meet Norman.

I was talking on the phone with Karen Stringer. "We call him 'Normie'. He's the ghost of a director who used to work with the theater. He died unexpectedly when he was quite young." It was late February 1960, and Norman Endean was just 34 years old. The photo that ran with the obituary shows a very handsome young man with dark hair and kind eyes looking dreamily off into the distance, a half-smile curving his lips, lost in his own imagination.

"Norman's a trickster," Karen told me. Props will go missing, then reappear – or not. And it's not only props. Someone who was working on costumes went to use the bathroom and found, to her dismay, that every roll of toilet paper was gone. Grumbling under her breath, she stomped off to get a roll from the supply closet. When she came back, she found a full roll of toilet paper sitting innocently in the stall she had just left, right where it was supposed to be.

Norman seems to have an affinity for the bathrooms. Another story says that he likes to hang out in the women's dressing room, often flushing the toilets. A large painting of him hung in the green room until October 2008, when it mysteriously disappeared. It hasn't been seen since.

"Come over to the theater sometime," Karen said lightly. "Someone will be happy to show you around."

It would be another month before I could find the time to visit the theater. I spent the month wavering between excitement and nervous anticipation. I had already been to the haunted asylum in Bartonville on a midnight ghost tour, but this would be very different. In Bartonville, I had been with a large group of eager ghost hunters, including my husband and two of my best friends. At the theater, though, it would be just me and the ghost.

The day I visited the theater for the first time was bright, sunny, and blissfully warm for the beginning of March – the complete opposite of my experience in Bartonville. I went in and introduced myself. Karen came out of the box office to take me backstage. As we walked through the hallway, I learned some more about the theater. Peoria Players Theater is the oldest continuously running community theater in Illinois. It's been going since 1919. Everyone I spoke to seems pleased that the theater has its very own spook. The company even gives out the "Normie Awards". I asked Karen what the awards were given for, and she said they are general pats on the back for good work in making props, or directing, or anything really.

"So it's kind of an 'Attaboy' award. Or 'Attagirl'."

Karen smiled. "Yeah, exactly."

By that time we were in the backstage area. It was dark, and I was starting to get nervous all over again.

"Let me get someone to turn on the house lights for you. That'll light up the backstage too." Karen gave me a level look. "You can stay back here if you want, nobody will mind, but I'm not staying with you."

Oh boy. What does she know that I don't? I thought. Nervously, I stuck close to the open door, and the safety of the bright sunny hallway beyond, until the house lights came up.

I peered around the backdrop, a huge curved shell of wood and canvas marked with the casual graffiti of dozens of actors, mementos of their time on the stage (including the wistfully curious "Is that you, Norman?" in wide red brushstrokes). The backstage area was lit by a soft yellow glow, which now seemed welcoming rather than threatening.

Okay, you've been psyching yourself up for this for a month now, I told myself. *You're not going to chicken out now.*

"Hello Norman," I squeaked. Then I cleared my throat and tried again.

"Norman, I'm a writer, and I'm working on a book of ghost stories. I've been hearing lots of stories about you, and you seem like a really fun guy." (Hey, I figure ghosts like a bit of flattery now and then too.) "I'd really love to tell my readers that you're here, that you actually exist. Now, I don't have a bunch of fancy ghost hunting equipment with me, and I'm about as sensitive as a brick, so if you want me to know that you're here, you're going to have to make some kind of noise for me. Can you do that?"

I listened. Nothing.

"Norman, can you make some sort of noise for me, please?"

Not a sound.

I decided to try something different. I looked around for something light – something that could easily be moved by someone who happened to be made of ectoplasm. There was a child-sized desk sitting next to the backstage entrance, and on the desk was a stack of about a dozen small plastic cups, about the size of shot glasses. Ah-hah! I plucked the top cup off of the stack, walked to the middle of the backstage area, and put it down on a narrow pine board that was sitting on a waist-high platform. The cup was highly visible against the light yellow wood of the board, and I figured I could easily see it if it moved.

"There you go, Norman," I said, backing up a step and gesturing to the setup. "If you're here, please move the cup for me, okay?"

The cup remained stubbornly motionless.

It was at about that time that I was joined backstage by Sharon, who has been the props chair at the theater for thirty years, and Pam Stinson, a painter who also works on props. Sharon had tracked down a portrait of Norman – an 8x10, much smaller than the painting that's been missing since last October – and she propped it up on the chair of the desk. I gazed at the dramatic black and white photo, frowning as I tried to figure out why the man in the picture looked so familiar.

"He looks like a young Sean Connery," I mused aloud as the resemblance sank in.

Sharon grinned. "I've always thought so too." Sharon has had her own experiences with the movie-star handsome Norman. She has been up on a ladder painting a set, and has come down the ladder to find her paint can moved, sometimes all the way across the stage.

Pam had stories to share, too. Her first meeting with Norman came before she even knew there was a ghost in the theater. She was painting a set piece that was lying on a tarp on the floor, and she kept hearing noises around her – a rustle on the catwalk here, the thump of a board falling over there. She calmly took a break from her painting and strolled up to the box office, where she asked her co-workers, "Is it just me, or do other people hear weird things too?" That's when she found out about Norman. Satisfied that it wasn't "just her", she went back to work. The soft noises started again. Quietly, Pam said, "Norman, if you're interested, just come and look."

Moments later, the plastic tarp across from her crackled, as though someone had just stepped on it to peer more closely at her work.

Pam told me that Norman's presence doesn't scare her. "It's just noises," she said, mostly the sharp crack of wood on wood, as if someone is selecting boards for building a set. And when people in the theater are talking, and the conversation turns to improvements to the building or to things the theater needs, the noises get louder, as if Norman approves.

We talked for a while. Pam pointed out the catwalk where Norman has been seen, and the disco ball that turned itself on one night before a singalong.

I glanced at the clock. It was getting late – time for me to get back to my day job. Pam and I walked backstage, where the cup still sat, untouched.

"Okay Norman, I have to go. If you want to let me know that you're here, this is your last chance, 'cause I'm leaving."

Pam stared at me, her eyes wide. "Did you hear that?"

"No!" The word came out as a frustrated yelp. Did I mention that I'm as sensitive as a brick?

Pam pointed up at the catwalk to our left.

Nerves singing, I spoke again. "Norman, that was great, but I didn't hear you. Can you make another noise for me, please?"

Pam whirled and pointed up to the catwalk to our right, just as I heard a noise – so faint I couldn't tell what it was, but definitely a noise. Then I heard another faint noise up on the left catwalk, and then again on the right.

"Oh, thank you, Norman! Thanks so much!" I was ecstatic – I'd talked to a ghost, and he'd "talked" back!

And because I was raised properly, and because I'd been taught to put things back where I found them, I picked up the lone plastic cup from the platform and turned back to the desk to put it in its place on top of the stack…

…but the cups weren't there.

Now, I'm notoriously absent-minded, but I knew there had been a stack of cups there. I knew it because I clearly remembered taking the top cup off of the stack for my experiment with Norman. The picture of Norman, black and white and broodingly handsome, was still propped up on the seat of the desk, but the stack of cups was gone.

I looked at Pam, utterly baffled for a moment. "Did you…there was…did…okay, there was a stack of plastic cups, just like this –" I held it up – "right here. Did you – you didn't move them, did you?"

Pam shook her head, amused at my stuttering. "Nope."

I'd been expecting that. I knew she hadn't moved the cups, because she'd been with me the whole time. A goofy grin spread across my face as it sank in. The trickster had gotten me good! I told Pam about the experiment I'd set up, and she started laughing along with me. "That's Norman for you. He'll always do what you least expect him to.

"But to be fair, you *did* ask him to move the cup!"

Two weeks later, I came back to the theater with Shari, one of my best friends, and her digital camera. If Norman decided to show up again, we were determined to get a picture of him.

Another theater employee, Jim, had told me about a photograph, taken from the stage, that showed a shadowy version of Norman sitting in one of the theater seats. This echoes a story Jim told me about Wayne, a lighting director, and Wayne's five year old son. Wayne was in the light booth setting the lights for a show. His son was in the booth with him, peering down into the theater from his high-up perch. The kid pointed down at the seats. "Daddy, who's the man sitting down there in the theater?"

Wayne looked out of the wide light booth window to see only empty seats below.

Jim says that Norman can be quite helpful at times. Take the disco ball, for example. Norman also turns on stage lights from time to time.

"So would you say that Norman's ghost is pretty active?" I asked Jim.

"Oh yes. He's very active, but he does keep his own schedule. A couple of weeks can go by when things are quiet, then two or three people will say they've seen or heard something weird."

I'd been warned that sometimes Norman lays low for a while, which was why I was disappointed, but not surprised, when Shari and I failed to see or hear any sign of Norman during our visit that afternoon.

But Norman is not alone in the theater. There is another spirit that dwells there, a darker entity, one that likes to play mean-spirited tricks on unsuspecting humans. A ghost-hunting group called GUARD, which stands for Ghost Unit – Analysis Research Detection, has investigated the theater. The EVPs (electronic voice phenomena) that they captured during one evening's ghost hunt were quite disturbing. In one, a rough, deep voice says "Get out!" In another one … well, this is a family book, so I can't tell you what the other message was. When I heard those EVPs, though, I knew the voice couldn't belong to sweet, gentle, funny Norman. I knew there was another ghost in the building.

One night, I came to the theater with my friends Gail and Allie, as part of the newly minted ghost research group RIP, or Research in Paranormal. We were there to join MAGH (Mid-America Ghost Hunters), led by Anne Prichard, in an investigation of the theater. Gail and Allie and I chose to work with Anne for the entire time we spent there. During the second half of the investigation, Anne announced her intention to do EVP work up in the workroom behind the stage, in the back corner of the building.

"Ohhh, rats," I groaned. "I really, *really* don't want to go up there. We're going lights-out for this, aren't we?"

"Of course," Anne said as we walked to the back of the theater.

"Yeah, I knew it," I sighed. Since we had agreed to work with Anne, I knew I had to suck it up and go up there. As we climbed the raw wooden stairs up to the workshop, ducking to avoid braining ourselves on the low metal bar at the top of the stairs, I explained my reluctance. The nasty entity has been known to concentrate itself in this corner of the building. Months before, when I had been in the theater very late at night with Pam and a couple of friends, Pam had gone into the back corner by herself. She came back out in a hurry, holding onto her composure with both hands. She told us in a low voice that something back there had breathed on her in the dark – and that breath had been deathly cold.

The four of us – Anne, Gail, Allie and I – settled into rickety chairs in the tiny, cramped, cluttered space. I took a deep breath, closed my eyes, and clicked off my flashlight.

My eyes sprang open in the darkness. I felt twitchy-uncomfortable, like I wanted to jump right out of my skin. "I don't like this," Gail muttered. "I don't like this at all." Gamely, Anne clicked on her digital voice recorder and started the EVP session. We asked a few hesitant questions, while I sat, tense in every muscle, terrified at the thought of what might be hovering around us in the black unknown.

Gradually, though, I calmed down. It seemed as though my mind was adjusting to the darkness, just as my eyes were. I found that I could breathe more deeply and easily, and the cold hand of fear clenched around my stomach loosened. "I'm starting to feel better," I mentioned. Across from me, Gail murmured "Mm-hmm," then fell silent. I could still catch some unknown, unidentifiable movement out of the corner of my eye, off to my right, at the front of the stage. It looked like a tangled, snarling ball of dark, frustrated energy. But whenever I turned to look, there was nothing there. I was still a little nervous, but whatever-it-was was way up at the front of the stage. Somehow I knew it wasn't coming any closer than that, so I relaxed a bit.

Later, on the way home, Gail filled me in on what had really happened up there.

"When you said you were feeling better, that was when Norman came in and drove the other entity away." Gail is much, much more sensitive than I could ever hope to be. "It was like Norman came and ordered the bad spirit to leave, and made a circle of protection around us. The other spirit was still there, but it couldn't get to us – it was off to the far right." Exactly where I had sensed irritable, impotent movement. "Didn't you feel it? Norman forced the other entity to leave. That's when you started to calm down. Norman was there with us, and that circle of protection – well, it was centered on you. Don't you get it?

"Sylvia, Norman *likes* you."

Haunted Houses

Having someplace to go is home...having someone to love is family...having both is a blessing. Maybe that's why so many ghosts haunt the houses in which they lived. Happy memories, memories of safety, security, and love, can draw spirits back to the places they knew in life.

Mike Waldron lives in a beautiful house on a winding road in East Peoria. It was one of the first houses built in the area, and it looks for all the world like a great big beautiful red barn. I pass it often on my way to work at the college, and before Mike told me his story, I'd have never guessed it was haunted.

"My room's down in the basement. I get the supreme privilege of being down in the dungeon," Mike told me with a rueful grin. He has seen a shadow person walking down the basement stairs. He says he can make out the figure of a short old lady with curly, iron-gray hair. "You remember the actress from that old show 'Mama's Family'? That's what she looks like, no kidding."

There are other strange things that happen in that house, nothing constant, just random weirdness. There is a painting, Mike says, that will tilt itself out of true every once in a while. He has photographed orbs down in his basement room, orbs that appear as white spots with a faint orange border. He has also seen a short man wearing overalls and a trucker's hat. According to EVPs Mike has recorded, the old woman is Darcy, and the man in the hat is her husband (Bill or Bob).

The haunting at Mike's house seems to be residual, and fairly tame as hauntings go. But his sister Amy had her own haunted house experience in Peoria, when she lived in a house on Perry Avenue. For her, the ghostly experiences were quite a bit more startling.

Amy told me that one day, she had just gotten home, and was met by her uncle, who said, "Oh hey, I just saw you coming up the stairs." Confused, Amy replied that she hadn't been up the stairs to the second floor yet – she had just barely walked in the door.   Her uncle said, "I could have sworn it was you. But wait – I saw someone in a white outfit." He frowned. Amy was wearing a dark blue shirt and jeans.

At that moment, Amy happened to glance out the screen door to the patio outside. "I saw an old lady out there. She looked like she was setting the table for lunch – and she was dressed in white."

As if this wasn't disconcerting enough, Amy told me that in that house, her family also owned a haunted piano. They had gotten the antique piano from an aunt in Chicago. Every so often, tinkling notes would sound from the instrument – not a recognizable tune, but random notes, "as if our cats were walking on the keys" was how Amy described it to me. Oddly enough, the piano was badly out of tune, but when phantom hands played these impromptu songs, the notes were clear and tuneful. Amy and her family moved two weeks after taking possession of the piano.

They did not take the piano with them when they moved.

Anne Prichard, of MAGH, told me of a haunted house that her group investigated in Pekin.

When the owner of this house was a little girl, she and her family had lived across the street. Her parents knew the former owners well. It was an elderly couple that owned the house, and they were good neighbors to the young family across the street. The husband eventually passed away in the house. His wife moved to a nursing home, and died some time after her husband. Their house was put up for sale, and the girl's parents decided to buy it, moving their family across the street. The young girl grew to adulthood in the new house, and now lives there with her own children.

The woman's daughter – let's call her Annika – has lupus. One night, she was suffering with a particularly severe attack. She was lying in bed, clenching her teeth against the pain, when she became aware of a woman standing by her bed. The woman had red hair, and was wearing bright red lipstick. But her most distinguishing feature was her hands, gnarled and knotted with arthritis.

The old woman held up her afflicted hands. "I know you're in pain, my dear. I'm in pain too." She smiled at Annika. "I'll tell your mother. She'll be in to help you soon." Then the woman faded from sight.

Annika's mother did come in shortly, and Annika asked her about the ghostly visitor. Her mother – "Joan" – had been too young to really remember the former owners of the house in which she'd grown up. But in response to Annika's questions, Joan asked her own mother about the old couple who had owned the house previously. Joan's mother remembered her old across-the-street neighbors well, and even had a few photographs, which she dug out and showed to Joan and Annika.

Annika's description of the kindly red-haired woman matched the long-dead neighbor perfectly.

My friend Christy has had her own ghostly encounter, which she shared with me. Several years ago, her grandmother passed away. She had been a strong woman, a personality that had held the family together. One night soon after her passing, Christy was lying in bed, remembering her grandmother, and wondering sadly how the family would carry on without her.

Christy gradually became aware of a presence in her bedroom. She opened her eyes, and realized that there was a shadowy figure standing at her desk, which was near the foot of her bed. She felt no fear, only a sense of overwhelming peace and security. She knew immediately that her grandmother had come for one final visit.

The figure hovered near the desk for a few moments. Then it moved closer to Christy's bed, to her dresser. Christy kept a few precious keepsakes there, including a necklace given to her by her grandmother. The figure paused at the dresser, as if examining the contents of Christy's jewelry box.

Then the figure drifted over to Christy's bed. It lingered at her bedside – perhaps saying a final goodbye to her cherished granddaughter. Then it faded away, becoming just another one of the shadows in the darkened room.

"It was my grandma," Christy swears. "I know it was her, and no one can ever tell me any different."

Tales Out of School

Louis Vargas (name has been changed) backed out of the open elevator door, pulling the bulky floor polisher out of the elevator. He just had this one last hallway floor to buff, then he was done for the night.

He set up the polisher, then paused, his finger over the "on" button. Movement out of the corner of his eye had distracted him. Louis had heard the stories about the high school, of course. He had heard of the teachers leaving messy piles of papers on their desks, to come in and find that the papers had been stacked neatly overnight. Sometimes, the papers were even graded. He knew there was something spooky going on in the quiet, darkened hallways, after the bustle of the day had faded.

Louis looked up to see a man standing halfway down the hall. The man looked like a teacher, although he was here awfully late. He was watching Louis with a stern, critical glare. The man frowned, then shook a finger at Louis warningly.

"Get to class!" he growled in a gruff voice –
then vanished!

Building A of the East Peoria High School is
a warm, red brick building, standing in cozy
contrast to the cooler sand color of the newer wing
of the school. Stained glass suncatchers wink from
some of the windows, with hanging plants peeking
from behind their glassy colors. The popularity of
the school sports team is obvious by the large gold
and maroon billboard at the corner of the campus
parking lot, and by the "Go Raiders!" signs
displayed at various businesses around town. From
the outside, the building looks welcoming, with a
friendly academic feel to it.

And on the inside, some of its teachers still
roam the halls, even after their deaths.

Before her retirement, Judy Murphy was an English teacher at the high school. She used to go in on Sunday afternoons to grade papers in the calm of the weekend. One quiet Sunday, she was unlocking her classroom door when she happened to glance down the hallway. Through the glass windows of the double doors, she saw the former art teacher step out of a classroom and bend over to light his pipe.

"I was so glad to see him again that I didn't even stop to consider that he'd been dead for years," Judy told me. She delightedly called out, "Jack!" and headed down the hall for a visit with her old friend. As soon as she burst through the double doors, though, there was no one there.

"I knew it was him," Judy said. "The classroom he'd come out of wasn't the classroom he had taught in while he was alive, but I knew it was him because of the pipe. That slight bend at the waist as he lit it – that was such a characteristic gesture. In fact, his wife had tucked his pipe into the pocket of his suit jacket just before the casket was closed at his funeral."

While Judy's ghostly experience was pleasantly melancholy, rather than unsettling like the stern disappearing teacher that Louis saw, she worries about the future of these spirits. There are plans to demolish A Building, and that bothers her.

"If they tear down the building, where will those poor ghosts go?"

Cohomo

Does a tall, white, hairy relative of Bigfoot
live in the woods and fields around East Peoria?

The legend of a primitive ape-like creature
in this area started back in the late 1930s. The
woods around East Peoria, and Pekin too, are home
to several coal mines. A walk along Lick Creek in
Pekin will still turn up pieces of coal, some as big as
your fist. Cole Street in East Peoria is named for the
numerous coal mines in the area, as is Coal Miner's
Park in Pekin. Mining companies worked the area
in the mid-1930s, but most of the mines were
abandoned by the end of the decade. Many people
think the old abandoned mines could be home to
monstrous creatures. And in 1950, a farmer near
Princeville reported that something had devoured
fifty head of livestock and poultry. The farmer said
he had heard a loud roar, and had come outside to

find his livestock slaughtered. He later found tracks that he said were as big as a man's hand.

But it was in the summer of 1972 that the legend really took off.

July is prime berry picking time in this part of Illinois. Black raspberries tumble in wild profusion along roadways and in hidden hollows in the woods. Anyone brave enough to dodge thorns, spiders, bumblebees and nettles can get a pail full of berries for jelly fairly quickly. One Pekin woman's berry picking plans, though, were abruptly cancelled. On July 20, 1972, she was out by an old coal mine on Route 98, three miles east of Route 29, when she saw the monster. She didn't give a description of what she'd seen, but she was so frightened by it, she ran off, leaving everything behind.

Three weeks earlier, at the beginning of July, the reports of monster sightings had begun rolling in. The creature was nicknamed "the Cole Hollow Monster", or "Cohomo" for short, because many of the sightings seemed to come from the area at the bottom of Cole Street called Cole Hollow. More than two hundred calls jammed the switchboard at the East Peoria police department. The police threatened to administer lie detector tests to anyone filing a monster report. The callers reported seeing an ape-like creature, anywhere between eight and twelve feet tall, covered with white hair, and moving in its own sulphurous cloud of stink. One witness said he had heard the monster roar – "It let out a long screech, like an old steam whistle, only more human." Two "reliable citizens" said they had gotten a fairly good look at Cohomo. They said it had long grey U-shaped ears, a red mouth with sharp teeth, and thumbs with long second joints, and that it looked like a cross between an ape and a caveman.

The description of the beast should have been enough to give anyone second thoughts about wandering around after dark in the hot summer nights. But on July 7, that's exactly what a bunch of people did. About a hundred people from East Peoria and Creve Coeur went out with flashlights, armed, to wander Cole Hollow Road in search of the creature. The monster hunt ended when one man accidentally shot himself in the leg with his .22 pistol as he was stepping over a log.

Cohomo seems to have laid low for a while after the monster hunt. But in the summer of 1986, another witness reported a strange encounter. Fran Roark said she was driving a little VW up Cole Hollow Road, with a friend in the car, when the headlights went out and the car died. The VW rolled back down the hill to the parking lot of the brickyard. It was about 11 pm on a dark night that was filled with the soft sounds of a summer evening – a light rainy drizzle hitting the leaves, the scuffle of some small animal in the underbrush, the constant soothing chirping of tireless crickets. Roark and her friend sat in the car for about fifteen minutes, talking quietly before they tried to start the car. Gradually, they realized that the crickets had stopped chirping, and that everything had suddenly fallen breathlessly still. Then they noticed a foul odor engulfing the car. Roark later said that it smelled like a cat that had been run over three days ago.

Eerie noises came from the dark woods behind the brickyard, a shrieking wail that got louder as they listened, as though whatever-it-was was coming closer. Their nerves broke, and Roark and her friend stumbled away from the car and ran down the hill to a friend's house nearby. When they got to their friend's house, they found a welcome, but not much comfort – because the friend had had a similar experience of her own.

In April of 1991, it was revealed that the Cole Hollow Monster was a hoax, dreamed up by a bunch of teens to scare one of their friends. Randy Emert called the Peoria Journal Star after the paper ran a story about a woman who had a run-in with Cohomo. The woman told East Peoria police that the monster had grabbed the bumper of her pickup truck on the 500 block of Cole Street and prevented her from driving away. Randy was seventeen when he and his friends made up the monster story. They'd all thought it was funny until someone ended up shot during the mass monster hunt.

But if it was a hoax, what did the woman picking berries in 1972 see? What scared the VW driver on that rainy summer night in 1986?

And what grabbed the bumper of the woman's truck?

For the Incurable Insane

It was late at night in November, and bitterly cold. The weather had been mild for fall, but it had changed that week, and now winter was here with a chill promise of things to come. I was at the abandoned, shuttered insane asylum in Bartonville, along with several friends. We were there to hunt ghosts.

We all shivered in our heavy jackets as we gazed up at the darkly forbidding building. The Bowen Building, one of the last standing structures of the asylum, is constructed from large sand-colored blocks of stone. No glass remains in any of the windows, and the empty windows on the bottom floor are covered with weathered gray plywood boards. The whole building gives off a chill air of menace, even on the hottest days of summer. Here, at night with the breath of winter making us shiver through our coats and gloves, the building seemed alive with the unknown.

It wasn't always so. When Dr. George A. Zeller took over management of the asylum in the early part of the 20th century, he tried to better the inhumane conditions for the residents. He often pointed out that if someone treated a dog or a horse as badly as some of the patients were treated, they'd be arrested for cruelty. As the director of the Peoria State Hospital, as the asylum was then known, he chose inmates from asylums all over the state, bringing the worst cases to the hospital for humane treatment.

One of the patients at the asylum was a woman known as Rhody, who had lived for 43 years in the Adams County almshouse. She was demented, deformed, and blind, having gouged her own eyeballs out during a fit. She had also knocked out all of her teeth. Her limbs had atrophied, because for years she had been confined, first in a straw basket, then in a box-shaped bed. Rhody had once been quite beautiful, and in her teens, had been engaged to a farmer's son. The boy's family, though, was opposed to the marriage. His mother visited Rhody and threatened to bewitch her if she didn't agree to break off the relationship. This drove Rhody insane, and she did seem to develop symptoms of possession. She was committed to the Adams County Almshouse, and later came to the Peoria State Hospital.

Dr. Zeller prided himself on hiring staff that would treat patients humanely, without the need for restraints. This included both physical restraints and the use of harsh drugs and sedatives. He took out all of the "restraint apparatus" and removed the bars from the windows and doors. His reasoning was that if a patient was used to being at home, where perhaps not even the front door was locked, it would be harmful to put them in such a restrictive environment. Dr. Zeller felt that it was the job of the attendants to keep a close eye on the patients, not just lock them up. Instead, Dr. Zeller used the iron bars as the boundaries for a deer park on the grounds for the enjoyment of the inmates. The patients were encouraged to feed and care for the animals. In one corner of the deer paddock stood one of the dreaded "Utica cribs", a small cage for locking up violently deranged patients. (Rhody had spent many years confined in such a crib.) The cage now held rabbits.

   The deer paddock and the caring attendants are long gone. Only the empty rooms of the Bowen Building remain, their doors torn off, their floors littered with rotting two-by-fours and crumbling drywall. Perhaps the tortured spirits of the former inmates roam these halls as well.

Our ghost tour started in the basement, which had at one time housed the morgue. This happened to be my very first ghost tour, so I was on edge the whole time, not knowing what to expect. (Hey, every ghost hunter has to start somewhere.)

When we were all gathered around the guide in the hallway next to the open door of the morgue, the guide told us we were going "lights out". This means turning off the flashlights. *All* of the flashlights. For someone like me, who nurses an irrational but life-long fear of the dark, this is like saying, "We're going to the aquarium – yay! And when we get to the shark exhibit, we're going to strip down to our skivvies and just hop right on in there with them, how's that sound?" I shivered and closed my eyes, seeking darkness on my own terms before the lights went out.

Click. The last flashlight was shut off, and we stood there, silent in the darkness. A strange sound came from somewhere down the hallway, and I gasped. "Are you okay?" the guide murmured.

"Yeah, fine," I muttered back. I wasn't about to admit how unnerved I was at the sound. As we were all standing there, listening hard in the utter blackness of the basement, I had heard a soft cooing moan, like the sobbing call of a pigeon, but without the trill. When we turned the flashlights back on, I apologized to the guide for startling, and explained the noise I'd heard that had made me gasp.

"I heard it too," he said, his face serious.

We climbed the concrete stairs, which were filthy with plaster dust, up to the attic. As with most of the building, the floor in the attic was too fragile to safely support the weight of dozens of people per night walking on it. So we were restricted to a small area at the top of the stairs. The rest of the attic was blocked off with waist-high sheets of plywood, giving us a clear view to the other end of the building.

We went lights-out again. "Watch closely," the guide whispered. We looked out towards the other end of the attic. An EXIT sign glowed redly in the darkness. As we watched, the red glow of the sign faded into the blackness, then reappeared moments later, just exactly as if some dark phantom had crossed the hallway in front of it.

On the third floor, we encountered more strangeness. Again, the main part of the hallway was blocked off by plywood boards, so that we could see the debris-filled floor, but not walk on it. The dust lay thick on the floor, proving that no one had walked there for years. Our guide asked the familiar question: "Is there anyone here? If you're here, can you make a noise for us?"

From the middle of the hallway, up against the far wall, we all heard a quiet *"tap...tap...tap...tap...tap...tap..."* Then it stopped.

"Can you do that again for us, please?"

Tap ... tap ... tap ... tap ... tap ... tap ... tap ...

Twice more, the mysterious taps repeated when we asked them to, seven or eight slow, measured taps at a time, then silence. We couldn't agree on what could be making the steady noise. Some people said it sounded like the ticking of a large grandfather clock. Other people swore it sounded like a steadily moving rocking chair, or like a child skipping rope. To me, it sounded like someone rapping a cane against the floor. Whatever made the noise, though, we all agreed that the tapping was meant to communicate with us.

As we made our way down another flight of stairs, I turned to a friend who, years before, had gone into the asylum after dark to explore. This was a favorite pastime for some adventurous teens, and the risk of getting caught by patrolling cops only added to the allure.

"So, when you guys were hanging out in here, crawling through tunnels and stuff, did you ever hear any weird noises?"

"All the time," came the calm reply. (This friend of mine is not easily flustered. Or spooked.)

"What did you do when you heard weird things? Did you ever think it was ghosts?"

My friend shrugged. "We always just assumed it was other kids out here making as much noise as we were. We just went the other way."

"Old Book"

The most well-known story associated with the asylum at Bartonville is the curious case of Old Book. We know of this strange, eerie episode from the writings of Dr. Zeller himself.

Some of the residents suffered from not only mental illness, but from physical weaknesses too. Decrepit old age, heart disease, pellagra, epilepsy, tuberculosis – the list of fatal illnesses was just as long within those stone walls as it was out in the world. Many of the inmates ended up buried in one of the four graveyards on the property.

A grave would be dug, the simple coffin lowered into the hole, then a short ceremony would be said over the departed. It was the deceased's fellow inmates who had the somber chore of digging the grave and lowering the casket. One of the residents, an elderly man known only as Bookbinder, was overcome with emotion at every funeral he attended. "A. Bookbinder" had come to the asylum unable to speak coherently. All anyone knew about him was that he had once worked in a printing house. Dr. Zeller wrote that at every funeral Old Book went to, the scene was the same – and Old Book never missed a funeral. "First his left and then his right sleeve would be raised to wipe away a furtive tear but as the coffin began to descend into the grave he would walk over and lean against the big elm that stood in the center of the lot and give vent to sobs that convulsed his frame and which could be heard by the entire assemblage." Old Book's mourning tree became known as the Graveyard Elm, and it was always the site of his weeping fits.

In time, Old Book himself died. He had become well known at the asylum, and several hundred people attended his funeral. This huge turnout made what happened next even more spectacular. As the choir finished singing "Rock Of Ages", four inmates took hold of the ropes to lower Old Book's coffin into the grave. But when they heaved on the ropes, the coffin was yanked up as if it were empty.

"In the midst of all this commotion a wailing voice was heard and every eye turned toward the big elm whence it emanated. Every man and woman stood transfixed, for there, just as had always been the case, stood 'Old Book' weeping and moaning with an earnestness that outrivaled anything he had ever shown before," Dr. Zeller wrote later.

The coffin lid was pried up by hands that fumbled with haste and fear. The wailing stopped in an instant, and there in the coffin was Old Book, lying with his hands folded across his chest. He was unmistakably dead.

Dr. Zeller wrote of the incident, "It was awful but it was real. I saw it. One hundred nurses and 300 spectators saw it."

Old Book was buried, but the story wasn't quite over. Within weeks, the stately old Graveyard Elm started to wither. It died despite frequent watering. When the time came to take the dead tree down, though, it refused to go. A groundskeeper tried to cut it down, but threw his axe down after the first stroke, saying that the tree had screamed in agony. Later, a fire was built to try to burn the tree down, but t.._ ..emen controlling the blaze soon put it out. They said that the roar of the flames sounded exactly like Old Book's moaning. One of the men even said that the trailing wisps of smoke came together to form the face of Old Book.

"Don't Touch!"

Practically everyone I spoke to in the area had a tale to tell about Bartonville. Some of these stories come from before the asylum's closing, when patients still lived there. The lady who cuts my hair said that when she was going to grade school in Bartonville, sometimes a patient would wander away from the grounds. Very often, the wandering inmates would find their way to the grade school and stand at the windows, looking in at the children. Were they remembering happier hours as they watched children at play?

A friend's uncle – we'll call him Greg – told me that when he was young, his Boy Scout troop would volunteer at the asylum. He said he was kind of nervous about going there, but that the attendants were always on hand to prevent any incidents. On Greg's very first visit, though, he had an experience he would never forget.

The attendants encouraged the patients to socialize with each other. Games, visiting, and other activities were permitted, because it made for a sense of community among the patients. One patient, though, kept to himself, rocking and muttering, looking down at his lap as his fingers fidgeted incessantly, drumming an insistent rhythm on his kneecap. The Boy Scouts were warned, "Don't touch Jonesy."

Well, one afternoon the Boy Scouts were there doing their volunteer visit, and Greg saw Jonesy sitting in the hallway all by himself. He looked so lonely sitting there, Greg said, that he just forgot about the no-touch rule. He went up to Jonesy, bent down a little to look into the lonely man's eyes, and he said, "Hey, Jonesy, how're you doing today?"

And then he put his hand on Jonesy's shoulder.

Jonesy's head came up with scary speed, and his rheumy blue eyes fixed on Greg's clear brown ones. Greg backed away slowly, not sure what the old man was going to do next. The glint in Jonesy's eyes, and the slow grin that spread across Jonesy's face, were making him very, very nervous.

Suddenly Jonesy lunged towards Greg, one liver-spotted hand outstretched. Greg's nerve broke, and he turned and ran. He ran down the hallway, and at the door he stopped and looked behind him. Jonesy was still coming. He yanked open the door and ran into the stairwell. He clattered down the stairs, looking up when he got to the bottom.

Jonesy was still coming.

Greg slammed his hands against the exit bar and escaped into the open air. He took big, gulping, panicky breaths as he backed away, his eyes on the slowly closing door. Movement behind the glass caught his eye. Jonesy was still coming.

The soles of Greg's Air Jordans slipped on the grass as he spun to escape. He ran across the wide lawn in front of the asylum and down the sloping hill. He ran across the street at the bottom of the hill, then he ran across the train tracks that stitch their way along the banks of the river. Every time he dared to glance behind him, he saw Jonesy running close, panting hard, but still gaining, because Jonesy was still coming!

Greg's breath came in harsh, hard gasps. He had reached the river's edge. Brown water washed the sandy strip of beach, lapping at the shore. There was nowhere left to go, and Jonesy was still coming. Greg looked wildly around, and saw a tree a little ways from the water. One of the branches was low enough to reach, and it looked strong enough to hold his weight. Greg jumped for the branch with both hands. He got a good grip on the rough bark, and hung there, his feet dangling. He just couldn't get enough leverage to pull himself the rest of the way up.

Jonesy came around the edge of the treeline. He saw Greg hanging there, and his grin got wider. He hobbled over to where Greg dangled helplessly from the branch. Cackling, he grabbed Greg's ankle with one gnarled hand, and cried out in a reedy voice –

"Tag! You're it!"

"Who Ya Gonna Call?"

Allie yawned as she drove home that night. Her class at Bradley University in Peoria was a late one, and she was definitely dragging after a long day. She squinted against the bright lights of Auto Row as she passed the half-dozen car dealerships on the way into Pekin. Then the glaring lights faded into the normal glow of streetlamps. Allie sighed. She was going to be so glad to get home and get to bed.

Soon she was passing the cemeteries that lined both sides of the road. She shivered slightly as her car's headlights glanced off of the polished granite of the headstones that crowded up against the busy street. Allie's gaze was drawn to the oldest part of the cemetery, on the right side of the road, before the monument showroom.

She blinked. That wasn't right. There was a mist, like a miniature patch of fog, floating among the headstones. Route 29 runs along next to the Illinois River. Pekin Lake is nearby too, just across from Auto Row. So Allie had driven through fog plenty of times on her way home from Peoria. But this…this was weird. This didn't look like any fog Allie had ever seen.

Eyes front, she gripped the steering wheel. "It's just fog, it's just fog," she chanted under her breath.

But as she drove past the baby cloud, it started to follow her.

Allie snatched up her cell phone. With one hand on the wheel, she dialed the phone with shaking fingers.

At the McDonald's in town, up Court Street, Gail's phone rang. The heroic notes of the theme from Indiana Jones blasted into the air, adding to the noise in the kitchen. Gail fumbled the phone from her pocket and jammed the "talk" button with her thumb.

"Yeah, Allie? Whaddya need?" Without waiting for an answer, she held the phone away from her ear for a moment to yell at one of her employees. "The North Pekin store want to borrow some grape tomatoes? Well, tell them they can have 'em, but someone has to come and get 'em. We're a little busy right now."

"Mom, something's following me."

"What? Honey, I didn't catch that. We're really getting slammed here, I've got both drive-thrus backed up, and –"

"Mom! Did you hear me? I'm driving past the cemetery, there's this creepy mist stuff, and it's following me!"

"Well, just…just drive faster, sweetie."

"Mom, wait, don't hang up! Don't –"

Gail clicked the phone off and slipped it back into her pocket. Almost immediately, it rang again. "Dahn-dah-dahnt-dah, dahn-dah-dah!" She snatched it up and thumbed "talk".

"Allie, I am busy here! Didn't I tell you that?"

"But Mom, it's –"

"Look, Mommy's the manager of the busiest McDonald's in Pekin, and she doesn't have time for – hang on a sec. Hey! This is *McDonald's*, pal. We don't *do* flame-broiled. I see flames on that grill again, you and me are gonna have words."

"Mo-om! I'm almost nineteen years old! Quit treating me like a kid! I'm not imagining this, and I'm not making it up! Seriously, it's still following me!" Allie risked a glance out the passenger-side window. The mist was still pacing the car at 35 mph, weaving in and out and between headstones as it went. As she watched, one hand in a death grip on the steering wheel, the other pressing the phone to her ear, eyes wide with disbelief, the mist reached out a wispy – arm? *tentacle*? – and floated closer to the car.

"Aaugghh! Mom! I gotta go!" Allie shrieked. She tossed the phone into the passenger seat, grabbed the steering wheel, and floored it, hoping there wasn't a cop waiting for her up ahead. At the Sheridan Road light, she had to slow down, then stop for a red light. There were houses here, with warm yellow light spilling from their windows.

The parking lot of the Busy Corner restaurant was full. She had left the cemetery a few blocks behind her. Hopefully, she'd left…whatever it was…behind her too.

Her breath still harsh in her throat, Allie forced herself to look out the passenger side window. There was no sign of the mysterious, spooky mist that had chased her – that had reached out for her! The house on the corner had two full garbage cans sitting out, ready for the next day's pickup. That ordinary detail, that simple reminder that life went on, really calmed her down, and she started to breathe easier. She was safe, and whatever had chased her was back in the cemetery where it belonged. The light turned green, and Allie started to move. Once again, she was just a tired college student on her way home.

She still couldn't believe that her mom had hung up on her. That, thought Allie, was something she was never, ever going to let Gail live down.

Hazel

The town of Tremont is a cozy place. It's the home of the annual Tremont Turkey Festival in mid-June. The festival is a welcome to summer that includes carnival rides, games, a parade, and loads of indulgent food, including all the turkey you could want halfway across the year from Thanksgiving. It's a small town, with a population of only 2,070 – and perhaps a few more.

There is a complex of government-type buildings located just outside of Tremont. Tazewell County Animal Control is here, Veterans' Assistance, other assorted county buildings – there used to be a Children's Home here too – and the Tazewell County Health Department. That's the one we're interested in.

Before the old health department building was torn down, employees there sometimes saw the filmy shape of a woman wandering the halls, dressed in a flannel nightgown. The prowling entity was also blamed for other disturbances in the building. Doors opened and closed by themselves, lights flickered for no reason, toilets flushed without a human hand on the handle.

The ghost was said to be that of "Hazel", one of the many former residents of the building. Before becoming the headquarters of the county health department, the building had previously been a nursing home for the county's indigent citizens. Hazel, and many others, lived out their lives in the building, then were buried in a nearby potter's field when they passed on. The poor farm closed in 1976. The following year, the health department moved into the building.

Gordon Poquette, a former director of the health department, had his own experiences with Hazel, beginning soon after his department moved into the building. He and an assistant were working on the budget one evening. This was in the late seventies, and they didn't have computers to make the task easier. Poquette and his assistant were poring over a table spread with sheets of paper, when they both heard thumps coming from the floor above them. "It sounded like someone with a wooden leg stomping around up there," was how Poquette described it to me. He went up to the floor above to investigate, but found no one. He came back down to continue his work. When he and his assistant both heard the mysterious thumping footsteps again, they decided it was time to knock off for the evening.

The old building was torn down in the early 1990s, but Gordon Poquette feels that Hazel simply moved to the new building, which was built close by. Before the old building was demolished, Poquette and local ghost hunter Rob Conover toured the building, and documented their evening on videotape. The famous psychic Greta Alexander spotted Hazel on the tape, in the form of a distinct orb. After viewing the tape, Alexander told Poquette that the spirits would move with him to the new building. "You'll experience electrical problems," she told him, "as well as automotive problems."

Soon after moving into the new building, Poquette told me, a rack of lights came crashing down. A leak in the roof above them had weakened the ceiling, and down they came. Also, several of the department's vehicles suffered unexplained flat tires. It seemed that Greta Alexander was right, and that Hazel had indeed followed the health department to their new home.

The Ghost of Duncan's Mill

Greed. Violence. Murder. Powerful words, powerful emotions. Spirits are drawn to high emotions, and sometimes, in a place where life violently tips over into death, they can remain to play out the drama for years afterward.

In 1889, two men sat shivering in the ruins of Duncan's Mill on an early spring night. They had heard the stories, and had decided to do some ghost hunting. They sat on a low stone wall, huddled against the frosty chill of the April air and the darkness of the night. One of the men pulled a pocketwatch out to check the time. It was nearly midnight.

A terrified scream split the night. "Don't, Jack! You can have the money! Don't –" The words trailed off into a strangled moan, the hideous sound of a throat that had suddenly filled with hot blood. The men glanced at each other, frozen with fear.

Then a skeletal figure appeared in front of their staring eyes. Its throat was sliced, and ghostly blood poured from the wound as the specter scrabbled uselessly at the gaping flesh. The ghost shrieked again, its unearthly voice a horrid gurgle. Blood spurted from between its skeletal fingers. The wraith staggered back and took a few tottering steps towards the ruins of the old mill, vanishing between the leaning, cobwebby beams. The two ghost hunters stumbled to their feet and ran, seeking the safety of nearby Lewistown.

The story of the tragedy at Duncan's Mill had started many years before, and was well-known in the area. According to local legend, two men were fishing near the ruins of the mill when they began to argue over money. The fight escalated, and one of the men attacked the other, slamming him over the head with a boathook and crushing his skull. To make sure of the job, the murderer then slit his victim's throat. Then he fled, leaving the boat and the battered, bloody corpse behind. The murderer was never caught, and the dead man was never identified. His body was simply buried near where he was found.

Soon after the murder, people who lived near the old mill started to mutter, saying that the place was haunted by the unfortunate victim. They said that on quiet nights, you could hear the gurgling screams of a man being slaughtered. Sometimes, the ghost of the doomed man would appear, trying desperately to stem the gush of blood from his fatal wound. The dead man of Duncan's Mill did not die gently, and he does not rest easily.

Havana Hauntings

If you ask any local ghost hunter if they've ever had any experiences in Havana, chances are they'll smile knowingly and nod. And chances are even better that they'll then mention two buildings in Havana: the Park District Gymnasium and the Lawford Theater.

The gymnasium seems to be haunted by the ghost of a young man. The kid had just finished a game of basketball and went downstairs to use the restroom. Somehow, he got locked in. Twenty-four hours later, his dead body was found, still trapped in the bathroom. It is believed that his ghost continues to haunt the gym, looking for someone to play one last game of basketball with him.

Anne Prichard, of Mid-America Ghost Hunters, says that the first time she went on an investigation at the gymnasium, her group heard some very strange things on their recording equipment. They had come into the gymnasium building, and had shut and locked the doors securely behind them. As they were setting up their equipment in the basement, they heard a door slam – the very door they had just locked! Even stranger was the fact that this noise was captured on the audio tape, but not on the audio portion of the video recorder.

The strangeness continued. In a storage room, the investigators were met with a feeling of oppressive evil. A whisper on the tape muttered, "Get outta here!" And in the gym itself, the researchers captured the distinctive sound of a basketball being dribbled on the polished wooden floor.

The Lawford Theater sits proudly in the middle of Havana's sleepy business district. In these days of multiplex cinemas, of blockbuster movies shown on five screens at a time, the Lawford is a reminder of a simpler age. Its glory days are behind it, but its faded wallpaper and worn seats still stand as silent testament to its former grandeur.

Anne Prichard will readily admit that there is "something" there. Her group was at the Theater for a training event, where researchers practice and hone their skills. The trainer had gone onto the stage to plug in some of the equipment that was to be used that night. He reported hearing three quick footsteps nearby, and then a voice that said, "Hey!" near his ear as though someone wanted his attention – but he was alone on the stage.

The old building has several levels of basements and sub-basements. The researchers took some audio recorders down to the lower basement. It's very common practice, during a paranormal investigation, to ask the entity to move something or to make a noise to let the researchers know of its presence. In this basement, there was a window partly covered with hanging, tattered plastic, white with age. Anne started the recorder, then asked, "Will you please move the plastic?" There was no response, so she left the recorder running and went back upstairs.

Ten minutes later, the noises began. The plastic over the closed window rustled, as if moved aside by an unseen hand. Then footsteps trudged up the basement stairs. Then the door at the top of the stairs slammed. Ordinary basement noises? Not when all the researchers are upstairs, and the basement is empty...

On another visit, Anne's group caught the sound of a circular saw running. The sound showed up on their audiotapes not once, but twice. The investigators had seen a saw sitting in the basement, so the noise was not completely unexpected. What made the noise unusual was that the saw wasn't plugged in!

Joanne Bridges, of the paranormal research team GUARD, was at the theater for an investigation. She was asking questions, carrying on a one-sided conversation, all in an attempt to capture EVPs. At one point, she said, "We're not here to hurt you," then waited. She heard nothing at the time. But on the audiotape, a whispered "*NO!*" came in answer.

"I wasn't scared during my first visit to the theater. But after getting home, and hearing that '*NO!* on the tape, you can bet I'm gonna be nervous when I go back!"

A Close Call

"See that open water up there, boys?"
Denton Offut said, spitting over the side of the
flatboat. "We're comin' up on the Illinois. We hit
that, we're on our way south to the Mississippi.
Then it's smooth sailing all the way to New
Orleans."

Offut's tall, lanky friend grinned. "That
means we kin unload these hogs, and that'll be jes'
fine with me." He looked out over the water.
"Looks like there's a pretty good crosscurrent
runnin' out there. It's rippin' right along, ain't it?"

Offut reached up to clap his friend's broad
shoulder. "You kin handle it, Abe."

Abe Lincoln nodded, his homely face set in
concentration. He eased the flatboat out onto the
wide waters of the Illinois, leaving the shallow
Sangamon River behind.

"Whoo! She's moving better in this deeper
water, Offut." The flatboat was loaded with barrels
of meat and produce, and dozens of squealing hogs.

The river caught the heavy boat and carried it
swiftly along.

"Look boys, Beardstown! Don't blink or
you'll miss it, the way we're racing along now!"
Offut yelled. Two boys were fishing off of the large
dock that thrust out into the water, kicking their
bare feet as they sat grasping the skinny poles. One
scrambled to his feet and hollered a greeting,
waving his whole arm at the flatboat as it churned
past. Lincoln lifted a hand from the tiller and waved
back.

Abe took a break from manning the tiller
near dusk to eat some supper. It was John Johnson's
turn to cook, and the smell from the beans
simmering with bacon and onions in the iron
cookpot was almost too good to bear after a hard
day of working on the river. Denton Offut took his
turn at the tiller while Abe filled his plate.

"Lookit the way we're zipping along," he
said, giving the steering pole a gentle nudge to keep
the boat straight on course. "We keep larruping
along like this, we'll make New Orleans by May."

John Hanks mopped up the last of his bean gravy with a crust of corn dodger. "Yeah, and here I thought we was finished when we fetched up on that dam at New Salem." He laughed and shook his head. "I still can't believe how you fixed that, Abe."

Offut slapped his knee. "Right you are! This here boat was stuck halfways over that consarned dam, and takin' on water to boot. If it'd been anybody else but you, Lincoln, who had suggested we unload the boat and drill a hole in it to let the water out, I'da called him a fool or worse. But here we are, floatin' merrily down the river, none the worse for wear." He stomped his foot on the deck, making one of the pigs squeal its irritation.

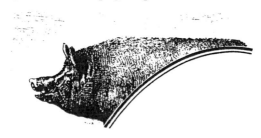

Johnson stacked the dirty plates and poured hot water into a basin. "Give us a story, Abe, to make the work go faster," he said as he started to wash the plates.

Hanks nodded. "You do the best yarnin' of anybody I ever met."

Offut pulled a flask of whiskey from his coat pocket, took a swig, and handed it to Lincoln. Abe passed it on without drinking, then leaned back against the deck rail and hooked his thumbs through his suspenders.

"Well, you know that whiskey can oftentimes get a body in trouble. I heard tell once of three fellers that were off visitin' a friend and stayed out real late, talkin' and drinkin'. Well, they were all three staying at a hotel in town, and 'long about midnight, they started back to town from their friend's house. Two of them hadn't tipped the bottle all that much, but the third one, he was feeling no pain atall. This third feller, he just kep' shambling along slower and slower, 'til he plumb got left behind.

"Now between their friend's house and the hotel was a cemetery. This ole boy was jes' so befuddled with likker, he went through the cemetery 'stead of going around it, and he stumbled and fell right spang into a freshly dug grave. He tried and tried, but he was in no shape to climb outen that hole. So he curled up right there in the dirt and slept the night away.

"The next morning, when he sobered up, he raised up and looked out around him. A negro was coming along through the cemetery, singing, with a basket of bread for the hotel balanced on his head. The feller, bein' the neighborly sort, said, 'Hello, and good mornin' to ye!' from the grave. The negro threw his basket right down and took off runnin' from the 'haint'.

"The man figgered the bread was for the hotel, so he climbed out of the grave, picked up the bread, put it back in the basket, and took it to the hotel. There he saw the poor negro he near 'bout scared the life out of, lookin' like he would faint, and telling ever'one about the ghost he'd seen in the cemetery in broad daylight."

Abe smiled at his friends, who were laughing fit to bust at his story. John Hanks wiped tears from his eyes.

"I'da been skeered too if someone had riz up outta his grave and told me 'howdy', wouldn't you, Abe? Abe?"

But Abe was peering out onto the bank of the river, shading his eyes against the setting sun and the gathering shadows. "If that don't beat all..." he muttered. He turned to John Johnson.

"Quick, John, you got anything for dessert?"

Johnson nodded. "I made a dried-apple pie. I was saving it for breakfast tomorrow, but you kin have it now if you want."

From his post at the tiller, Denton Offut snorted. "Thought I hired a boathand, not some fancytown baker."

"Quiet!" Abe snapped. To Johnson, he said, "Hand around that there pie, John." Abe stole a quick glance at the bank. "Yep, it's still there all right," he said to himself.

"Come on, John, give a big ol' piece of that pie here." Abe took a big slice of pie, cradling it in his huge hand. He took a great big bite and chewed. A piece of apple, plump, sticky, and dark with cinnamon, clung to his lower lip, and he licked it away. As he chewed, he motioned to the others to do the same. Abe swallowed and said in a loud voice meant to carry, "Yes sir, that's the best pie I've ever eaten! Sure does put a shine on a meal."

Offut hesitated, the pie halfway to his mouth. He stared towards the riverbank. "Dear God…what *is* that thing?"

"Eat, man!" Abe barked. "That shadow you see, deep among the trees – the shadow that's been keeping up with us for the past few miles – that's a wendigo. It's an old Indian spirit. It's the embodiment of hunger. Worse than that…it's the spirit of starvation. And if it touches you…" He shuddered, and his voice held a chill. "If it touches you, you turn cannibal. You become just like it, eating and eating and never bein' full, ever."

All four men looked over at the riverbank. In the last fading light of the day, they could see the wendigo. It was a dark, shadowy form, dressed in tattered rags that floated out behind it as it moved. Its skin was a sickly yellowish-gray film stretched tightly over its jutting bones.

"Look at it *move!*" Hanks breathed. "It's keepin' up with the boat – and we're goin' downstream! And it's so blasted tall!"

Abe nodded. "They say it grows bigger accordin' to what its last meal was, so it's always hungry, never satisfied." He held up his piece of pie.

"We ain't a-skeered of you! There ain't nobody starving here, not on this boat, so you jes' go off and leave us be! G'wan now, git!"

The wendigo's sunken eyes blazed yellow against the deepening shadows. Its skeletal arms reached out and it clutched at the empty air, as if seeking sustenance. Then it opened its mouth and let loose an eerie, hollow moan. There was no human warmth under that ghostly voice, just a cold, raw shriek of aching hunger and desperate longing. It stopped, and the flatboat quickly drifted downstream away from the wendigo on the bank. But the monster's lonely howl still echoed across the dark water.

Offut shivered. "Light the lanterns stem to stern, boys, all we've got. And make sure they're good and full of oil, and the wicks trimmed proper. I want them blazing 'til sunup."

The Fiery Phantom of Diamond Island

The area of Illinois where the Illinois River joins the Mississippi is known fondly as "the land where the Great Rivers meet". Paranormal investigators have long noticed that many weird phenomena can be linked to the presence of running water nearby. Maybe this accounts for the many strange stories that circulate in this area of the state. Perhaps the meeting of these two great rivers sets up a unique thrumming, silent tremelo of energy. This energy may power not only hauntings, but also other supernatural happenings, events far outside the realm of everyday experience.

1888. A group of townspeople is gathered in a loose knot on the shore of the Illinois River. One or two of them throw uneasy glances across the water towards Diamond Island. It will be dark soon, and when darkness comes, they will all row over to the island and see what there is to be seen.

Alfred is kneeling in the sand, trying to get a fire started. A fire will bring warmth and comfort, and right now, he is badly in need of comfort. Nearby, Joshua is talking in a low voice with Davey. Joshua has his father's old flintlock rifle resting casually against his shoulder as he talks.

"Those boys were scared, Joshua," Davey is saying. "They were the first ones to see the spook light, back in '85. The story was all over town, you remember? They'd been fishing, late at night, and 'round about midnight, they were just about directly across from the island. Matter of fact, I believe they were at this exact spot. They looked over," Davey points across the river, "and saw a ball of fire shoot through the trees and then hang suspended above the treeline. Spooked 'em so bad they ran right home and woke up their folks, babbling about seeing this weird fireball. The younger one even swore he could see the faint outline of a face in the flames."

"Kinda hard to believe, ain't it?"Joshua agrees. "Everyone thought the boys were just making up tales. But then other folks started seeing

the same spooky ball of flame. Saw it once myself –
nope, twice, now that I think on it. Uncanny, it was.
And little Will was right. I could almost convince
myself there was a face on it." He shivers. "Alfred,
ain't you got that fire started yet?"

"At least I brought lucifers with me," Alfred
huffs. "Not my fault the blasted things won't strike."
He stands up and brushes the sand from his knees
with short, angry swipes.

"I'm just glad all of us out here tonight are
armed. I wouldn't want to go spook hunting with
anything less than my good old .45-.70." Davey
reaches behind him and pats the lever-action rifle
slung at his back. He nods to Joshua. "How 'bout
you? Why'd you bring that old thing anyways?"

Joshua grins. "Don't poke fun, Davey. Two thimblefuls of powder will get me a squirrel any day of the week. We've had good squirrel gravy every morning for the past fifteen years thanks to Annie here." He unslings the flintlock and points the long barrel at the ground.

"Here's another reason I like this gun so much," he says. He puts a touch of priming powder in the pan. Then he lays a small piece of charcloth in the pan and closes the frizzen. He thumbs the hammer all the way back and winks at Davey.

"Watch this." Joshua kneels by the fire pit, points the rifle out over the water, and pulls the trigger. Davey and Alfred both flinch, but there is no bang. Instead, there is a soft fizz, barely enough to attract the attention of the other men standing on the beach. The charcloth sparks, and Joshua cradles the rifle on his knees. Carefully, he takes the glowing bit of cloth out of the pan, and reaches for the shredded bird's nest Alfred has been using for tinder. He tucks the orange glow into the dry grass, cups it, and blows gently. Then he lifts the kindling and puts the burning tinder underneath.

"There's your fire, Alfred."

"Thank God." Alfred lays a few more small branches on the fire. As he does, he casts a look across the river. The trees loom silent and dark, as if they hide secrets. And they do.

Soon it is fully dark. The small fire on the beach does little to push back the night. The men row several boats across the river and run them up onto the island's dark shore. They climb out, each man with his weapon of choice. They are a ragtag bunch, armed mostly with guns, but there are clubs, knives, even a few pitchforks to be found. Old Gerald Manes, who used to be a captain in the war, even has his old cavalry saber with him. He draws it, and there is a soft snick of metal on metal as it clears the scabbard. The men stand rigid with tension, not sure which direction to explore first, not knowing what to expect in the eerie woods. The yellow light of their campfire, on the other side of the river, seems impossibly far away.

Suddenly, the skies above them erupt with a reddish-orange glow. A ball of flame bursts up through the trees as if shot from a cannon. It hangs over the group, twisting silently and ominously in the black sky. Red light pours down on the men, painting their upturned faces with a hellish glow.

Captain Manes breaks the silence with a shriek. He brandishes his saber. "Get it, boys!" he yells in his quavery old man's voice. The men aim at the fiery ball and unleash a fusillade of shot. Davey fires and cocks his lever-action, the smart "snick-snick" giving him the confidence to continue. Joshua aims and fires. He has only a few shots every minute, so he has to make his bullets count. Alfred is empty already, and he fumbles with the loading gate, trying to shove cartridges into his revolver with numb, shaking fingers. The other men aim and shoot, aim and shoot.

But the ball of flame just hangs in the sky, untouched by the storm of lead. Then – horrors! – it comes closer, closer to the terrified knot of men. Still silent, growing closer –

"*Run!*" someone screams. With one word, the huddle breaks into an explosion of bodies, each man running, scrambling for the safety of the boats and the river beyond.

The ball of flame plunges down, landing in one of the boats. The force shoves the boat off of the sand and it bobs crazily in the water. The men watch in terror as the ball of fire coalesces, transforms, lengthens into the shape of a man. The

figure is old and stooped. Joshua blinks in disbelief.
This cannot be happening. Balls of fire do not drop
from the sky into boats, then suddenly transfigure
into the shape of an old man wearing denim
overalls.

The old man stands in the boat for a few
long moments, leering at the men with a skeleton's
grin. The boat keeps drifting backwards, further into
the river. In a moment, the current will catch it, and
someone will be out one flatbottom. But the men all
stand frozen with fear. No one wants to wade out to
the skiff. No one wants to get any closer to the
phantom.

The old man glows from the inside. Flames
lick from his eyes and mouth, suffusing his skin
with an eerie glow. In moments, the fire consumes
him, and he curls in on himself, turning back into a
ball of fire. The flaming globe lifts into the air,
vaulting away above the trees, disappearing into the
mysterious darkness of Diamond Island.

Epilogue

And now your little boat has come to the end of its long trek down the Illinois River. I hope you've enjoyed the ride.

I'd like to thank all of the people who have contributed so generously to this little book. Thanks to everyone mentioned within these pages for sharing their stories with me, and to the members of RIP, GUARD, MAGH, and Infocus for inviting me along on their ghostly adventures. Thanks so much to Troy Taylor for his help, encouragement, and inspiration. Enormous overflowing buckets of love and thanks to Shari – she knows exactly why. Thanks also to Bruce Carlson, my publisher, who suggested the idea for this book even before knowing I was the perfect person to write it. And big thanks to the staff of Fondulac District Library for their help (and their patience!)

This book was such a joy to write! I found so many stories of ghosts and strange happenings along the Illinois River that I couldn't include them all. I hope you'll visit my Facebook page (look up Ghosts of the Illinois River). That's where I'll be putting up more stories – all the wonderful strange weirdness that couldn't fit between the covers of the book.

If you're interested in learning more about ghost hunting, feel free to visit the websites of the groups mentioned in this book: www.ripillinois.org, www.magh.biz, or Google "GUARD paranormal". And if you'd like to know more about the other writing I do, please visit me at www.sylviashults.com. I love hearing from readers!

Thank you so much for coming with me on this trip down the Illinois River. I know it was spooky at times – that's why it's good to have company in the dark places. And I hope you found a few things to chuckle at along the way too. I'm so glad you could join me, and I'm already looking forward to our next journey together. Until then –

About the Author

Sylvia Shults has worked as a librarian, Bookmobile driver flower seller, dancer and art model. Her Hobbies include wild food foraging, baking, making wines and cordials, and gardening. She is hopelessly addicted to classical music and reading. She writes both horror and romance, and is the first to admit that the line separating the two can be very fine indeed. She firmly believes that there is no such thing as too many projects, and is currently at work on her next novel. She lives in Illinois, practically right on the Illinois River, with her husband, two furry German Shepherd daughters, two rotten cats, and far too many books.

GHOSTS OF INTERSTATE 90 Chicago to Boston by D. Latham

GHOSTS of the Whitewater Valley by Chuck Grimes

GHOSTS of Interstate 74   by B. Carlson

GHOSTS of the Ohio Lakeshore Counties by Karen Waltemire

GHOSTS of Interstate 65   by Joanna Foreman

GHOSTS of Interstate 25 by Bruce Carlson

GHOSTS of the Smoky Mountains by Larry Hillhouse

GHOSTS of the Illinois Canal System by David Youngquist

GHOSTS of the Niagara River by Bruce Carlson

Ghosts of Little Bavaria   by Kishe Wallace

Shown above (at 85% of actual size) are the spines of other Quixote Press books of ghost stories. These are available at the retailer from whom this book was procured, or from our office at 1-800-571-2665 cost is $9.95 + $3.50 S/H.

Ghosts of Interstate 75	by Bruce Carlson
Ghosts of Lake Michigan	by Ophelia Julien
Ghosts of I-10	by C. J. Mouser
GHOSTS OF INTERSTATE 55 by Bruce Carlson	
Ghosts of US - 13, Wisconsin Dells to Superior	by Bruce Carlson
Ghosts of I-80	David youngquist
Ghosts of Interstate 95	by Bruce Carlson
Ghosts of US 550	by Richard DeVore
Ghosts of Erie Canal by Tony Gerst	
Ghosts of the Ohio River by Bruce Carlson	
Ghosts of Warren County	by Various Writers
Ghosts of I-71 Louisville, KY to Cleveland,OH	by Bruce Carlson

GHOSTS of Lookout Mountain by Larry Hillhouse

GHOSTS of Interstate 77 by Bruce Carlson

GHOSTS of Interstate 94   by B. Carlson

GHOSTS of MICHIGAN'S U. P.   by Chris Shanley-Dillman

GHOSTS of the FOX RIVER VALLEY   by D. Latham

GHOSTS ALONG I-35   by B. Carlson

Ghostly Tales of Lake Huron   by Roger H. Meyer

Ghost Stories by Kids, for Kids by some really great fifth graders

Ghosts of Door County Wisconsin   by Geri Rider

Ghosts of the Ozarks   B Carlson

Ghosts of US - 63   by Bruce Carlson

Ghostly Tales of Lake Erie   by Jo Lela Pope Kimber

GHOSTS OF DALLAS COUNTY	by Lori Pielak
Ghosts of US - 66 from Chicgo to Oklahoma	By McCarty & Wilson
Ghosts of the Appalachian Trail	by Dr. Tirstan Perry
Ghosts of I-70	by B. Carlson
Ghosts of the Thousand Islands	by Larry Hillhouse
Ghosts of US - 23 in Michigan	by B. Carlson
Ghosts of Lake Superior	by Enid Cleaves
GHOSTS OF THE IOWA GREAT LAKES	by Bruce Carlson
Ghosts of the Amana Colonies	by Lori Erickson
Ghosts of Lee County, Iowa	by Bruce Carlson
The Best of the Mississippi River Ghosts	by Bruce Carlson
Ghosts of Polk County Iowa	by Tom Welch

Ghosts of Ohio's Lake Erie shores & Islands Vacationland by B. Carlson

Ghosts of Des Moines County   by Bruce Carlson

Ghosts of the Wabash River   by Bruce Carlson

Ghosts of Michigan's US 127   by Bruce Carlson

GHOSTS OF I-79   *BY BRUCE CARLSON*

Ghosts of US-66 from Ft. Smith to Flagstaff   by Connie Wilson

Ghosts of US 6 in Pennslyvania   by Bruce Carlson

Ghosts of the Lower Missouri   by Marcia Schwartz

Ghosts of the Tennessee River in Tennessee   by Bruce Carlson

Ghosts of the Tennessee River in Alabama

Ghosts of Michigan's US 12 by R. Rademacher & B. Carlson

Ghosts of the Upper Savannah River from Augusta to Lake Hartwell   by Bruce Carlson

Mysteries of the Lake of the Ozarks   Hean & Sugar Hardin